Growing Pains

by
Joe Coleman

Watermill Press

Printed in the United States of America

Illustrations by Jim Odbert

ISBN 0-89375-829-9

Contents

The Secret Room

Norman was unhappy. Ever since his family moved, he felt that his life had gone straight downhill. He had no friends, no neighbors—nothing.

"You'll meet lots of kids when school starts," his mother had told him. "Washington High is an exceptionally good school."

"Yes, sure," said Norman. The summer was just beginning, and out here in the middle of nowhere, he wouldn't meet anybody.

They had moved from a big town to a farm in the country. The only thing Norman really liked about it was the old farm itself. It was huge! There was a big house with three stories plus a basement. There were barns and stables. It was the kind of place you could get lost in, and with no friends, that's exactly what Norman did.

Then Norman found the well. The well was out back, and a pump brought the water from the well into the house. Norman explored the pumphouse. He saw the hoses that connected the well to the pump. The well shaft was covered with a trap door and locked with a big, heavy-duty padlock.

Norman ran back to the house to get the old key ring that had come with the farm. There must have been about twenty keys on it. Norman returned to the pumphouse and tried the keys until he finally found the one that opened the lock. Norman took the padlock off and opened the trap door.

He felt the cool, moist air rush up as he shone his flashlight down into the well shaft.

It was so deep he couldn't even see the bottom, but he did see steps — iron stakes in the side of the well. Norman climbed into the shaft.

Ick, thought Norman as he grabbed the first iron stake. *It's covered with slime!* He wiped his hand on his jeans, and kept climbing down. Now the opening above looked extremely tiny and very far away.

*Norman shone his flashlight down into
the well shaft.*

But after a few more feet, Norman found something surprising. There was a room in the side of the well shaft!

It was a small room, but large enough for Norman to stand up in and move around. The walls were stained brown and covered with mud, but Norman knew he had made a great find. Here was a place that no one knew about except him — a secret room. Now he had something to occupy himself with for the summer — as long as his parents didn't find out about it.

He had an idea. *I'll get some boards*, he thought, *and run a power line down here. With an electric light and a chair, it'll be a great hideout!*

He climbed back up the well shaft. Then he took the key off the ring, locked the door, and put the key in his pocket. When he went into the kitchen, he hung the key ring by the back door. *No one will ever notice that the key to the well is missing*, he thought.

"What's gotten into you?" Norman's father asked that night. "You seem to be enjoying yourself today."

"Nothing," said Norman. "I've just been exploring the farm."

All the next day, Norman worked on his secret room. He covered the muddy cement floor with old boards. Then he brought down an old chair and some cushions from the attic. Finally he added a lamp, an old radio, and most of his favorite comic books. At last he was satisfied with his secret room.

Over the next few weeks, Norman really enjoyed his room. Every day, he sneaked out to the pumphouse when no one was looking. He unlocked the door, and climbed down to his secret room.

One rainy day, Norman went into his secret room and fell asleep. When he woke up, he had no idea how long he had been down there.

He quickly started to climb up the shaft, when a sound from above made him stop. Norman kept very still. He didn't want anyone to know he was down there.

"I wonder who left this trap door open?" It was his dad! Norman saw the shaft darken and heard a slam as his father kicked shut the door to the well.

Then Norman heard another terrible sound. He heard his father lock the padlock! The door was locked from the outside and Norman had the key. He was trapped, but he couldn't give himself away!

Suddenly, Norman looked down and saw a frightening sight. The water in

11

the well was rising! Norman thought of all the rain there had been over the past several days. Then he remembered the mud over the boards and the brown stains on the wall. *The room must fill up with water after a heavy rain!* thought Norman.

Norman panicked and rushed up toward the locked door. He started banging and yelling.

"Help! Help!" he shouted at the top of his lungs. "I'm trapped in the well! Somebody please help me!"

It's no good, he thought. *No one can hear me out here.* Then Norman knew that he'd better use his head.

Somehow, I've got to let them know I'm down here, he thought. Nobody knew about the secret room because that's the way he had wanted it. But now nobody would have any idea where to look for him.

He quickly climbed down to the room and found a foot of water now covering the floor. The boards were floating, and so were the radio, the chair, and everything else.

He grabbed his flashlight and shone it around. *How can I let them know I'm down here?* he thought.

Then he saw the rubber hose that carried the water from the well to the pump. He knew what he had to do. He got out his pocketknife and began to saw at the hose.

After a few minutes, he had made a small hole, and the water from the hose began to trickle out.

It seemed to be taking forever, but finally the hose was cut. Now, no water would reach the house. Norman hoped that when the water went off, his dad would come out to investigate. Norman settled down to wait.

It was a long wait as the water in the well rose above the entrance to his room. But then he heard a strange, deep voice above. "It must be the pump," said the voice. Norman heard footsteps above him in the pumphouse and guessed that the man must be the plumber.

"No" he heard the voice say. "The pump seems to be working fine so it must be the hose. I'll have to drive back to town and get some more. I'll come back first thing in the morning."

"No!" screamed Norman. "Don't leave! Get me out of here!" Norman expected the man to answer, but what happened then totally surprised him.

When the plumber heard a voice from the bottom of the well, he thought it was a ghost! He dropped his tools and ran in

*The plumber dropped his tools and
ran in a panic.*

a panic, yelling, "Ghost! Ghost! The well is haunted!"

Oh, no! thought Norman. *Now I've really had it.* Then he started yelling, "It's me—Norman! I'm trapped down here! Somebody help me!"

All he could hear was the sound of the plumber's truck speeding away. But then he heard footsteps and a familiar voice calling, "Who's down there?"

"Dad! It's me—Norman!"

"What are you doing down there?" demanded his dad.

"It's a long story, Dad," said Norman. "Can you get me out of here?"

"Yeah," answered his dad. "Let me get the key."

"I've got the key!"

"You what?"

The lock was solid steel, but luckily for Norman, the locksmith that came out to open the lock wasn't afraid of ghosts.

Norman heard the lock give and saw the door open. He was stiff from crouching in the cold, damp shaft, but he got out of there in record time.

"What were you doing down in that well shaft?" asked his father.

"I had a secret room down there," answered Norman. He could tell that his father was getting angry.

"Well," scolded his dad, "it was secret all right, and you almost scared that plumber to death!"

Norman's father was pretty angry, but the memory of that old plumber running away screaming "Ghost!" was too much for him. He burst out laughing and, after a while, a very cold and tired Norman joined in, too.

The New Boy

Sandra thought she had it made. How could it get any better? She was one of the most popular girls in school. That was why she was surprised when Ernie Newcastle asked her for a date.

Who was Ernie Newcastle? That's what Sandra wanted to know. Even though the school year had just started at Washington High, everyone knew that Sandra and Ned Samson, the quarterback, were going out. Sandra only went out with popular boys. And no one had ever heard of Ernie Newcastle. So why did this guy from her typing class think that she would go out with him?

It all started when Sandra's mother told her that someone wanted her on the phone. "It's a guy," her mother had said.

"Is it Ned?" asked Sandra.

"I don't think so," answered her mother. "I didn't recognize his voice."

Sandra answered the phone. "Hello?"

"Sandra, this is Ernie Newcastle."

"Who?" asked Sandra, pretending not to know who he was.

"Ernie Newcastle. I'm in your typing class."

"Where do you sit?" asked Sandra, hoping he'd get the message.

"Usually, right behind you," said Ernie. Sandra could tell that she had hurt his feelings, so she tried to be nicer.

"Oh," she said, "I remember. You wear glasses, don't you?"

"Yeah," said Ernie, "that's me. I'm new in town, and I haven't met many people yet. I thought that maybe you'd like to go to the movies with me Saturday night."

He must *be new in town*, thought Sandra, *if he doesn't know about Ned and me*. "I'm sorry," she said at last, "but I already have a date this Saturday."

"How about Sunday?" asked Ernie.

Sandra couldn't believe her ears. This guy didn't give up! "No," said Sandra, "I'm helping my boyfriend with his term paper this Sunday."

"Oh," said Ernie. "I get the picture."

"It was nice of you to call, though,"

said Sandra.

"Sure," said Ernie. "See you in class."

Sandra felt a little sorry for Ernie, but she had to admit, his call had given her a boost. But he should know better than to ask out one of the most popular girls in school.

This was the week before the first football game, so the coach kept the team at practice late. Usually, Ned called Sandra every night after dinner. Tonight he didn't call.

The next day in school, Sandra saw Ned on his way to class. "Ned," she called, catching up with him.

"Oh—hello, Sandra," he said. Somehow, Ned seemed more quiet than usual. They walked for a while in silence.

Finally, Sandra asked him, "How's practice?"

"Coach Sawyer's working us to death,"

said Ned. "He kept us at practice until seven-thirty last night."

"Is that why you didn't call?" asked Sandra.

"Yeah," said Ned. "See you."

Ned entered his classroom, and Sandra realized that she had to go all the way to the other end of the school for her class. She ran all the way, but she was still late.

As she entered the room, Ms. Parker, her typing teacher, said, "We'll let it go this time, Sandra. But next time you're late, you'll have to get a late slip."

"Yes, Ms. Parker," said Sandra, trying to get to her desk as quietly as possible. She was so embarrassed that she didn't even notice Ernie behind her as she sat down. Ms. Parker started the class, but Sandra's mind was a million miles away. Ned had never been so cold before.

Something was definitely wrong.

Suddenly Sandra felt everyone looking at her. She jumped. Then she realized that Ms. Parker had asked her a question.

"Sandra," demanded Ms. Parker, "will you please answer the question!"

"Yes, Ms. Parker, the answer is . . ." Sandra could feel her face turning red. She had been thinking about Ned and didn't even hear the question! Ms. Parker was strict. The whole class was silent. Everyone was waiting for her to answer the question.

"Oh, I've got it," stammered Sandra, stalling for time. "It's . . ."

Then Sandra heard a whisper coming from behind her. "Block style business letter," said the voice.

"Block style business letter," said Sandra, holding her breath.

"That's right, Sandra," said Ms.

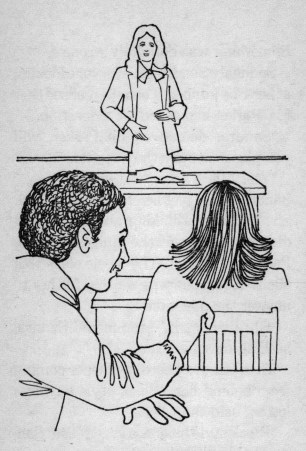

*Then Sandra heard a whisper coming
from behind her.*

Parker. "Now see if you can keep your mind off your social life for the rest of the class, and concentrate on typing!"

After class, Ernie followed her out of the room. Sandra was about to thank him for saving her when she saw Ned coming down the hall. She walked off after Ned without a word to Ernie.

Sandra felt relieved. Ned seemed like his old self again. He even invited her out to lunch. He almost never did that because he usually ate with some of the other guys on the team.

That night, Sandra felt better. She felt guilty about not thanking Ernie, but at least everything was all right between Ned and her. *And I can always thank Ernie tomorrow*, she thought.

She did thank Ernie the next day after typing class, and apologized for not doing it sooner.

"That's O.K.," said Ernie. "Is Ned Samson your boyfriend?"

"Yes," said Sandra, a little embarrassed.

"He's a good quarterback," said Ernie.

"I know," said Sandra, walking away. She wondered how Ernie knew that Ned was a good quarterback. The first game was still three days away.

That was Wednesday. On Thursday, Ned started acting strangely again. He was quiet, and there seemed to be something on his mind. Sandra felt as if she were riding a roller coaster, but she wasn't having any fun. The whole thing was making her upset.

On Thursday night, Ernie Newcastle called Sandra again.

That guy just doesn't get the hint, thought Sandra to herself when she heard his voice on the phone.

"How about a date a week from Saturday?" asked Ernie.

Sandra felt herself growing angry. With all the problems she had with Ned, she didn't need Ernie Newcastle bothering her. The last thing she wanted was a date with a nobody!

"Look, Ernie," said Sandra. "I'm really flattered that you keep asking me out, but the answer is no. You know that I'm going out with Ned Samson. Now please don't call me anymore."

Ernie said nothing for a moment, and then, "Sandra, are you sure you're going out with Ned Samson?"

Sandra couldn't believe her ears. What nerve he had! The question made her furious. "Of course I'm sure! Goodbye!"

Sandra hung up the phone and burst into tears.

On Friday, Ned was acting stranger than ever. He asked her out to lunch again and hardly said a word until they were sitting by themselves at a table.

Sandra couldn't stand it for another minute. "What's wrong, Ned?" she asked.

Ned looked at her for a second. Then he looked away. Finally, he blurted out some words that made Sandra feel like shrinking through the floor. "I've got another girlfriend," he said. "I'm sorry, but I'm going out with Shirley."

Sandra sat there trying to fight back the tears. Ned sat there, staring stupidly at her. Sandra wished he would get up from the table. She knew if she tried to say anything, anything at all, she would start crying. She was *not* going to cry in front of Ned.

Finally, as coolly as possible, she stood up and walked away. She kept herself from crying all the way to the girls' locker room. Then she sat down and let out the tears.

Now everything Ned had done made perfect sense to her. *That snake, Shirley*, thought Sandra, and then she started crying all over again. It wasn't until she thought of Ernie Newcastle that she stopped crying.

At least Ernie will be happy, she thought as she wiped away the tears. *Now I can go out with him*. Thinking of Ernie made her feel a little better. But she knew that getting over Ned and seeing him with Shirley would not be easy.

On Saturday, Sandra went to the football game with her friends. Since all their boyfriends were on the team, the girls always went to the games together. Today Shirley didn't go with them. Sandra knew why.

Everyone else already knew about Ned and her. To her surprise, Sandra found out that she was the *last* one to know about Ned and Shirley. But that wasn't the only surprise in store for her.

What really surprised Sandra was that Ernie was a running back on the football team. Ned and Ernie were playing together in the same game! Now Sandra knew why Ernie had asked her if she was sure she was going out with Ned. Ernie knew all about Ned and Shirley, too. He was Ned's teammate!

What's more, Ernie was really good! He ran with the ball over and over again. He even scored a touchdown. Ernie would not be a nobody after today. Sandra knew that the next time Ernie called, the answer would be yes.

After the game, she waited with some of her girlfriends for the players. Sandra

Ernie was a running back on the football team.

wasn't waiting for Ned, but there was somebody she was hoping to run into — Ernie Newcastle.

Just as she hoped, she saw Ernie leaving the locker room. He was headed her way! She forgot all about Ned.

But Ernie walked straight past her. He went right up to Judy! Judy smiled and the two of them started to walk off.

"Hi, Sandra," said Ernie. "See you in typing class."

Together, Judy and Ernie got into his car and drove off. Sandra went home and cried all night. These had been the worst two days of her life.

But through her tears, she had to admit one thing. She had been wrong not to go out with Ernie Newcastle just because he wasn't popular. That was one mistake she would never make again.

Her Big Moment

Meredith and Nancy couldn't wait for the school day to be over. Today was the day of the cheerleading tryouts and they had been practicing all summer long.

If they made the squad, Nancy and Meredith would see all of the games. They would travel with the team and get to know the players. Some of the players were really cute.

The last-period bell finally rang, and most of the girls at Washington High raced to the gym. The tryouts were about to start.

On her way to the gym, Meredith was in such a hurry that she bumped into the wall and dropped all her books. A tall boy bent over to pick up Meredith's things. "Good luck today," he said as he handed Meredith her things and walked away. Meredith blushed when she realized that the tall boy was Bob Baxter, the captain of the football team!

Meredith hurried to the gym and arrived there breathless. She found Nancy pacing outside with a worried look on her face. "I'm so nervous," Nancy said. "I really want to make the squad!"

"We'll just do our best," Meredith told

her as they headed to the locker room to change. They joined the other girls by the bleachers just as Susan Jones, the head cheerleader, called the group to order.

"I want to thank everyone for coming," Susan said. "We have three places to fill on the squad. We will also choose one alternate. Good luck to you all!"

Everyone groaned. Only three girls would be on the squad. The alternate would get to cheer only if someone got sick or something. But cheerleaders at Washington High never got sick.

Meredith and Nancy were very nervous, but they had worked hard for this day. They knew all of the cheers by heart. Pretty soon, it was Nancy's turn.

Nancy went to the middle of the gym floor. Her hands were trembling as she began her best cheer.

"E...A...G...L...E...S!" Nancy jumped high into the air and landed in a perfect split. Then she rolled into a somersault, leaped to her feet and ended with a beautiful cartwheel. The other girls cheered!

"Wow," Nancy said as she returned to stand beside her friend. "That was fun."

"You were great," Meredith said. Meredith wanted Nancy to make the squad because, during the summer, they had become close friends. Nancy had always been so shy, but now Meredith knew Nancy would be a great cheerleader and a wonderful friend.

Then, it was time for Meredith to try out. Meredith walked to the middle of the floor and began.

"1...2...3...4...Who are we cheering for? Eagles!" Meredith did a running flip, then leaped high into the air and

Nancy jumped high into the air.

came down in a perfect split. Meredith rolled into a somersault and came to her feet.

"Eagles!" she yelled, and everyone cheered. Meredith's heart was pounding. She had never done her routine better!

"You're the best so far," Nancy cried as she hugged Meredith. Then, they watched the rest of the tryouts. Most of the girls did not know the cheers as well as they did. Meredith and Nancy could hardly wait for the next afternoon. The new squad members would be announced in the gym.

The next day, the gym was packed. Everyone had come to hear Susan announce the squad. "It was a hard decision," Susan Jones said. It was very, very quiet. "These are the three girls who made the squad."

"Linda Morris," Susan said. Everyone

clapped for a moment, but then the gym got very quiet again.

"Dorothy Powers," Susan said, and everyone clapped again. Meredith saw Nancy tremble and squirm.

"Meredith Larson," Susan said. Meredith had made it! Everyone cheered, including Nancy. But there were tears in Nancy's eyes. Meredith felt good and bad at the same time.

"Our alternate is Nancy Rogers," Susan said. Meredith rushed over to Nancy.

"You made it," Meredith yelled. "You made it."

"It's only the alternate," Nancy said, but she felt better. It would be fun to practice with the squad.

The squad practiced for two weeks before the season actually began. Nancy came to the games, but she had to sit in the stands. After one of the games, Nancy and Meredith walked home.

"I want to cheer so badly," Nancy said sadly. "But I'll never get my chance. Never!" Meredith watched Nancy walk away.

I'm going to do something about this, Meredith thought. *Nancy deserves to cheer.*

Meredith went home and ran upstairs. She raced into her room and looked inside her closet. She pulled out some old crutches and some leg tape. *A sprained ankle ought to do the trick*, thought Meredith. *I'll tell Susan I have to stay off my feet for a while. This will give Nancy her chance.*

The next day at school, everyone gathered around Meredith. They wanted to know how she hurt herself.

"Uh...I...uh...tripped on a roller

Meredith watched Nancy walk away.

skate," Meredith said. She had taped her ankle the same way it was taped when she really had hurt her foot. She limped around school with her crutches.

"Meredith, I am so sorry," Nancy said. "Does it hurt much?"

"No," answered Meredith. Boy, was that the truth! Then Susan came up to Meredith and Nancy.

"We hate to lose you for a while, Meredith," Susan said, "but you've got an able replacement." Nancy's eyes widened.

"You mean—"

"Tomorrow night," Susan said.

Nancy grinned from ear to ear and jumped up and down.

"Save some of that for the game," Susan smiled.

"Oh, I will!" Nancy said gleefully. Meredith watched Nancy race down the hall. Meredith would remember this moment for a long, long time. Nancy would finally get her chance.

Then, Meredith felt a lump in her throat. She was going to miss cheering, even if it was only for just a little while.

I'll make a recovery soon, Meredith thought as she smiled to herself and began to walk home.

Walking with crutches was slow going. It was nearly dark by the time Meredith reached her house. As Meredith began climbing the steps, she felt something move under her left foot. Then, she felt a sharp pain in her left ankle as her foot twisted, and she fell with a thud.

"I'm afraid you've got a pretty bad sprain," Doctor Murdock said. "You'll have to stay off that foot for two or three weeks." Meredith just shook her head and laughed to herself as she limped out into the waiting area. Then she saw a tall boy sitting in a chair with two crutches—it was Bob Baxter.

"What happened to you?" asked Meredith.

"I got hurt at practice," Bob moaned. Then he saw Meredith's ankle. "You, too?" Bob asked.

"Me, too," Meredith said.

Bob cleared his throat.

"It looks as if we're both going to be sitting in the stands," Bob said. "Maybe we could sit together?"

"I'd like that," Meredith said, smiling brightly. The next three weeks would not be so bad after all.

The Pittsboro Stealers

That's right. We aren't the famous football team, the Pittsburgh Steelers. We're the famous Pitts*boro* Stealers. We live in a small town named Pittsboro. The real Steelers are our idols so we named our neighborhood football team after them. We used to just hang around and play football all the time. But now we're famous. We were even given a Good Citizenship Award! It happened like this.

A group of us—Eddie Gregory, Matt Bayer, Johnny Santucci, Vinny Silverman and I—used to hang out together after school. Usually, we'd meet at Johnny's house. He lives on a farm, and it's just perfect for playing football.

One day, we went down by O'Reilly's pond to play. We were there so long that, before we knew it, it had gotten dark.

We were headed for home when we heard a truck coming down the dirt road to the pond. Don't ask me why, but for some reason, we all hid in the woods.

The truck came into view. It didn't have its lights on. Eddie started to yell, "Mister, your lights are off!" But luckily, Matt stopped him before the driver heard.

We all hid in the woods and watched.

The truck backed up to the pond. The driver got out, looked around, and walked to the back of the truck. There was something very sneaky about him.

We couldn't see what he was doing, but, after a few minutes, we heard a big *splash*. A horrible smell filled the air.

Matt sneaked out of the woods to see what the man was doing. Matt took about three steps. But then the man came back around the truck! Matt dove for cover just before the driver saw him.

I just knew that the man was up to no good, so I got out my notebook and wrote down the number on his license plate, *AJK 341*.

After a while, the driver took one last look around and climbed back into the truck. We stayed out of sight until we could no longer hear the motor. Then we went out to get a closer look.

*Matt sneaked out of the woods to see
what the man was doing.*

"It really stinks!" said Johnny.

"Yes," said Eddie. "I wonder what it is?"

"I don't know," said Matt. "But I bet my dad would know." Matt's dad was a chemist at the factory.

Vinny found an old soda bottle and handed it to Matt. Matt was careful not to get any on his hands as he used an old rag to shove some of the smelly dirt and water into the soda bottle. Then he stuffed the rag into the top of the bottle. We promised to meet the next day.

The next day, we all gathered to hear the news. "What was that stuff?" I asked Matt.

"You won't believe it," Matt replied, "but there are traces of a dangerous chemical in that water.

"My dad told me it's one of the most dangerous chemicals known, and it's against the law to dump it anywhere!"

"What should we do?" asked Vinny.

"Well," said Matt, "my dad said we should take this bottle and the license number of the truck to Sheriff Mason."

"Let's go," I said. We all got on our bikes and rode downtown to the sheriff's office.

"What can I do for you, boys?" asked Sheriff Mason.

All together, we started to tell him about the truck, the driver, and the chemical in the water.

"Hold it!" he said. "One at a time, please!"

I described what we had seen and gave Sheriff Mason the license number. Matt showed Sheriff Mason the bottle with the muddy water in it.

"You boys have done a good job. I'll take the license number of the truck and have the lab look at this bottle. If this is what you say it is, you can be sure that *somebody* is going to be in big trouble!"

We all felt good about what we had done. We talked about it for days. But we never heard any more about it. After a while we just forgot the whole thing.

Early one morning about a month later, my mother woke me up and showed me the headline of the local newspaper, *The Pittsboro Weekly:*

LOCAL BOYS UNCOVER
ILLEGAL DUMPING SITE

"Wow!" I said. "That's us—the Pittsboro Stealers!"

When I got to school, I showed the headline to the other guys. While we were talking, Mr. Thomas, the principal of Washington High, walked up and told us to come with him to his office.

When we got there, we saw Sheriff Mason and another man.

"Boys," said Mr. Thomas, "I'm sure you all know Sheriff Mason. This gentleman is Mr. Filmore from the government."

"We've been after this illegal dumper for a long time," said Mr. Filmore. "Thanks to you boys, we've finally caught up with him. And thanks to your evidence, we can send him to jail. If it weren't for you, he'd still be dumping poisonous chemicals."

Mr. Filmore reached into his briefcase and brought out a large piece of paper. "We have decided that you boys deserve a reward. On behalf of the federal government, it's my pleasure to present you with this Good Citizenship Award."

He showed us the paper:

*Mr. Filmore reached into his briefcase and
brought out a large piece of paper.*

Awarded To

Richard Bunker
Edward Gregory
Matthew Bayer
John Santucci
Vincent Silverman

*In Recognition of the Good Job They
Have Done for Their Community.*

We all felt terrific. But we were in for even more good news.

"I think you boys deserve a little reward from me, too," said Mr. Thomas. "So take the rest of the day off."

We all talked it over and decided to head straight out to play football. Pittsboro is sure a lot better off thanks to a group of guys called the Pittsboro Stealers!

World's Greatest Dribbler

Mike Jackson knew it was going to be tough.

"Look, Jackson," the coach of Washington High told him, "basketball is a game for tall people. Nothing personal, that's just the way it is."

"Come on, Coach," Mike pleaded. "I

love basketball. Won't you even give me a chance?"

Coach Sawyer took a long look at the boy. He threw up his hands as if to say, "What can I do?" Then he gave in and said, "O.K., Jackson, suit up. Be on the court in five minutes."

"You won't be sorry, Coach!" Mike yelled as he ran to the locker room to change.

Mike Jackson was only five feet, six inches tall, much less than average for basketball players. But although Mike wasn't very tall, he felt he did have one advantage—he was the world's greatest dribbler.

In minutes, Mike changed clothes and ran out onto the floor. His friends Harry Franklin and David Collins were there. Harry was a great shooter, and Dave was very strong on defense.

"I hate to disappoint you," Dave said to Mike, "but if you try to dribble past me today, I'm going to have to steal the ball right out of your hands."

"Try it!" Mike replied, and both boys grinned.

"All right," announced the coach, "count off. You, on the end, start there!"

One by one, they counted off, "One, two, three, four, five . . . seventeen, eighteen, nineteen."

The coach looked at his clipboard. "I've got eight places on the team," he said. "You all know what that means. Before the day is over, eleven of you will be cut."

Everyone looked around at everyone else. Mike could feel the nervousness in the gym. There was no question about it —he was the shortest guy there.

At the start of the tryout, things

There was no question about it—Mike was the shortest guy there.

didn't go very well for Mike. No one would throw him the ball.

One guy kept trying to show off. Every time he got a pass, the player drove through to the basket and tried to sink the ball.

At last, the coach stopped the game and chewed him out.

"Hey, Presky," shouted the coach, "at this school we play basketball as a *team* sport! Have you ever heard of that before—a *team*? Now let's see a little teamwork out there!"

From across the floor, Mike saw Presky's face turn red. Presky passed the ball to another player and the game started up again.

After the coach gave his speech about teamwork, things became a little looser. Everyone tried to show how good he was at team play. Finally, after the other team scored, Mike got his chance. Harry Franklin threw him the ball, and Mike dribbled it down court.

Because he was short, Mike easily dribbled past the taller guys. He could weave in and out of traffic while they were just getting ready to bend down.

Mike took a quick look down the court. He could see a path to the basket through the defense. He faked to the left and started dribbling up the right sideline. Then Dave Collins came up to stop him. Mike was a little worried because Dave knew most of his tricks.

Mike looked down court, and saw Harry Franklin in position to move in under the basket. Mike's eyes met Harry's. They both knew the play.

Mike had only one chance. It was risky, because it was a fancy move. If it didn't work, Mike knew he would look like a fool. He decided to go for it.

Mike heaved a bounce pass right between Dave's legs. Harry knew just what to do. He made his move to the basket. *Swish*, he sank it!

Dave gave Mike a surprised look, and Mike shrugged his shoulders. Dave smiled and patted Mike on the back. "Good move, Jackson," he said.

From then on, the guys on Mike's team let him take the ball down court every time. As usual, Mike became the chief dribbler on his team. Now he had a chance to show off some of his fanciest moves.

Suddenly, the coach blew his whistle, and it was all over.

"I honestly have to say," announced the coach, "that I saw some pretty good talent out there today. You *all* need a lot of training and practice, but on the

Harry made his move to the basket.
Swish, *he sank it.*

whole, you're about the best group of freshmen I've seen.

"But I've only got eight spots so I had some hard decisions to make. The following players will be on the team this year."

Mike closed his eyes and tried to will the coach to say his name. *Come on, Coach,* he thought, *say Jackson, Jackson, Jackson!*

The coach read out the names, "Frank Holyfield, Steve Moscovitz, Fernando Rodriguez..."

Three down, Mike thought. *I still have a chance.*

"...John Osborne, Tony Stevens, Harry Franklin, Phil Jones, David Collins."

For a second, Mike couldn't believe the coach hadn't chosen him! What a letdown it was for him!

Then Mike heard the coach call his name, "Hey, Jackson!"

"Yeah, Coach?" he said, trying to sound cheerful.

"I saw you play some pretty good basketball today."

"Thanks, Coach. I work on my dribbling all the time."

"I'm not talking about your *dribbling*, Jackson," laughed the coach. "I'm talking about your *teamwork*. I like to see a player like you on the floor. You could really teach some of these hotshots a thing or two about team play!"

"I wish I could," Mike said, a bit confused.

"Well, I've been thinking about that, Jackson, and I've got an idea."

The coach was smiling, and Mike felt his heart pounding as he began to hope that he still had a chance.

"I don't have any more slots on the team right now," said the coach, "but why don't you come to practice anyway? Work out with the team, and help me show these guys a few things about teamwork. Who knows? There's usually a new slot or two by the time the season starts."

"Do you mean it, Coach?" Mike asked, not believing his ears.

"See you at practice, Jackson. Monday at 3:30."

"Right! Thanks, Coach! Thanks a million!"

Mike was now very confused. He had always *worked* hard on his dribbling. He had never thought about teamwork before. *I guess it just comes naturally to me*, he thought.

As Mike walked towards the door, he felt about ten feet tall. He heard the coach call him again.

"By the way, Jackson," said Coach Sawyer, "we've really got to teach *you* a thing or two. Those fancy tricks of yours come pretty close to double dribbling. It's a good thing there weren't any officials here today!"

"Ah, yeah...right, Coach," Mike stammered. "I'll see you Monday."

Mike couldn't believe it! He thought his dribbling would get him on the team! But if the coach wanted him for his teamwork, that was just fine with Mike.

Butterfingers

Mark Weber hated it when his friends chose sides for baseball. The two team captains were Eddie Harrison and Jim Jefferson. Harrison won the coin toss, so he chose first. He chose Kirk Smith. Everyone always picked Smith first, and Mark was always chosen last. As a matter of fact, everyone at Washington High called Mark, "Butterfingers."

That's why Mark hated it when they chose sides.

Mark watched them choose. Coach Sawyer, the gym teacher, looked on from the dugout.

Jefferson chose next. He looked at the group of boys standing around. "Chuck Nagle," called out Jefferson.

Nagle jumped up and ran over beside Jefferson. Now it was Harrison's turn to choose again.

Now Harrison looked at the group of boys. Mark could tell that he was having trouble making up his mind. Harrison looked at Sam Valentine and then at Paul Krebbs. Finally he said, "O.K., Valentine, you're on my team."

The two captains kept on choosing. Mark watched as the group grew smaller, and there were fewer and fewer players to choose from. Mark closed his eyes and hoped he wouldn't be the *very* last one chosen. He looked at the group.

He saw Bob Johnson. Johnson sometimes got chosen after him, but sometimes not. Mark crossed his fingers.

The two captains kept choosing until there were just two more players left to choose—Mark and Bob Johnson. It was Jefferson's choice. He looked at Mark and Johnson. "O.K., Johnson," he said.

Harrison, the other captain, didn't even wait to choose Mark. He and the other guys just ran to the outfield, and Mark ran with them.

Harrison said, "O.K., I'll play shortstop, and Smith will play first. Valentine, you play second base. Wetzel, play third. You other guys take the outfield."

Mark waited. He wanted to know *where* in the outfield.

"Come on, Butterfingers!" shouted

Harrison. "What are you waiting for? Head for the outfield!"

Mark ran out to left field. Now that the choosing was over and the game had begun, he felt a little better.

He stood in the outfield and watched as Paul Krebbs got up to bat. Sholar was pitching. Mark was so far away in the outfield, he didn't even feel as if he were playing in the same game.

Mark knew he usually got chosen last because he almost always struck out. And although he could throw the ball very well, he had a hard time catching it when it came to him. Once he got it, he could throw it out of the park, but he didn't get it very often.

On the second pitch, Krebbs hit a high fly ball. Mark hoped it wouldn't come to him. It came down in right field. Mark breathed a sigh of relief as Ferguson ran under the ball and caught it.

Jefferson was next at bat. Sholar threw the ball across the plate. *CRACK!* The ball sailed off Jefferson's bat. It was a hard line drive right at Mark. Mark threw his body in front of the ball and put out his hands. The ball whizzed right by him!

Mark heard the rest of the team groan as he chased the ball. When he got it, he looked at the field. Jefferson was rounding second. Mark knew he could make it to third. He threw it to Wetzel, the third baseman.

It was a beautiful throw, straight at Wetzel. Wetzel caught it and tagged Jefferson. The whole team yelled, "Jefferson, you're out!" Jefferson argued a little, but he knew he was out. He headed back to the dugout.

Harrison looked out at left field. "Nice

The ball sailed off Jefferson's bat. It was a hard line drive right at Mark.

throw, Butterfingers!" Mark felt good until Harrison added, "But you can't catch, can you?"

Now there were two outs. Sholar pitched one to Houston. Houston swung and missed.

But the next pitch was an easy lob that just glided across the plate. Houston swung and lined it right back at Sholar. Sholar didn't know whether to try to catch it or to get out of the way. Then it was too late. The ball hit him hard—right in the leg!

Houston headed for first, but the whole team ran in to see if Sholar was all right. He wasn't.

"How are you doing? asked Coach Sawyer. Sholar just rolled around on the ground, groaning. A few minutes later, he sat up and felt his leg.

Harrison helped Sholar up. He limped

around. He seemed wobbly. "I'll send Sholar to the nurse's office," said Coach Sawyer. "He can't play like this!"

The game got started again. There were two outs and Houston was on first. Harrison needed a pitcher to replace Sholar so he looked at the team.

"O.K., Smith. Why don't you pitch?"

"Sure," said Smith, "but who's going to play first?"

"Wetzel," said Harrison, "you play first; and Ferguson, you play third . . . ." Harrison stopped, and a light came into his eyes. "Wait one minute."

"Yes?" asked Smith. "Wait for what?"

"Hey, Butterfingers!" said Harrison. "Do you think you can pitch?"

"Who, me?" asked Mark.

The whole team started laughing. They thought Harrison was joking. "Come on," said Wetzel. "Weber? Be serious."

"I *am* serious. Didn't you see that throw he made to third?"

"That doesn't mean that Butterfingers can pitch!" said Valentine.

"I'm putting him in!" said Harrison, looking at Mark. "Well, Weber, what are you waiting for?"

Mark couldn't believe it. He never thought that anyone would ask him to pitch. He didn't know what to say.

"Well?" asked Harrison. "Can you or can't you?"

"Sure!" Mark heard himself say. "Sure, I can pitch."

"Not Butterfingers!" said Valentine. "I don't believe it!"

"Come on, you guys," called Jefferson. "Let's get this game going!"

Everyone took his place as Mark stepped up to the pitcher's mound.

Andy Simpson was next up at bat.

Mark knew that he could throw well, but he just never thought the others would let him pitch. Everyone on both teams was watching him. Valentine was shaking his head. Mark looked at Grossman, the catcher. Grossman looked back at him as if he couldn't believe his eyes. Mark took a deep breath and went into his wind-up. "Ball one!" called the coach.

Mark felt a little more relaxed after the first pitch. He started to believe that maybe, just maybe, he *could* do it. He wound up and threw it as hard and as straight as he could. Simpson took a mighty swing, but his bat just whizzed through the air. It was a strike!

"All right!" Mark heard Harrison say. "Do it again, Weber!"

Mark threw it again, but Simpson hit

a pop up to shortstop. Harrison made an easy catch for the final out.

Now Mark's team was at bat. They got two players on, but Wetzel popped out to third base, and no one scored.

Mark went back to the pitcher's mound. Bob Johnson was up at bat. Mark heard his teammates say, "Easy out." They moved in closer.

Mark felt sorry for Johnson because he knew how Johnson felt. Mark didn't want to, but he knew he could strike Johnson out. He wound up and threw a perfect strike!

After five pitches, Mark struck Johnson out. Mark heard his teammates cheering him on. "Way to go, Butterfingers!" Mark couldn't believe that he really struck someone out! He *was* good at something!

But Nagle, the best hitter of all, was

up next. Nagle looked up at Mark. "Come on, Butterfingers!" said Nagle. "I'm not an easy out like Johnson."

Mark got angry and pitched one near the outside corner. Nagle didn't swing. "Ball one!" the coach yelled.

Nagle laughed at Mark. Mark threw another pitch, but this time Nagle swung and missed. "Strike one!" shouted the coach.

Now it was Mark's turn to laugh. He threw another pitch, then another and another. Soon, there was a full count on Nagle—three balls and two strikes.

Mark had never had so much fun in all his life. He knew he could do this so he felt good, relaxed. But this next pitch was the all-important one.

He wound up and threw a fastball. Nagle's bat met the ball and sent a pop up, right to Mark.

The others groaned as they waited for Mark to miss the ball. They knew that Mark was a terrible catcher. But they didn't know something else. For the first time in his life, Mark *knew* he could do it. Before, he never *believed* he could catch it. Now he *knew* he could.

Mark saw the ball high above him. It looked like a little white speck in the sky. The ball hung in the sky for a moment before it began to fall. The little white speck got bigger and bigger.

Mark moved under it and put up his glove. *Plop!* The ball fell right into his glove and a cheer went up in the field.

"Hey, Butterfingers!" shouted Harrison. "Why didn't you tell me you were a good player?"

"I didn't know it myself," laughed Mark.

"Right!" said Harrison. "I believe that! We're going to have to change

*Mark moved under the ball and
put up his glove.*

your name to 'Fastball!' "

The game got going again. Mark felt as if he were the king of the world. He knew he wouldn't be the last one chosen the next time he played.

Then he looked at Bob Johnson.

Mark remembered how he had hoped that Johnson would be chosen last. He saw how badly Johnson felt sitting by himself in the dugout. Mark felt a little sorry that he had struck Johnson out.

Soon, Mark's team won. School was over for the day so the guys headed to Jayston's store for sodas. Mark started off with them. Then he saw Bob Johnson walking home all alone.

Mark hurried off after Johnson.

"Hey, Fastball!" said Harrison. "Aren't you coming with us?"

"Not right now," answered Mark.

Harrison and the rest of the guys

started off just as Mark caught up to Johnson.

"Hey, Johnson," said Mark. "Let's practice a little."

"What for?" asked Johnson. "You don't need it."

"Look, Bob," said Mark. "I know how you feel. Maybe we can both stop being the last ones chosen."

"But you had a great day. Why do you want to hang out with me?"

"Come on," said Mark, "let's practice. If I can do it, so can you."

"Do you really think so?"

"I not only *think* so, I *know* so!"

Mark Weber and Bob Johnson played catch until it got too dark to see. Bob couldn't throw and Mark couldn't catch. But they kept getting better all the time as long as they believed in themselves.

The Show
Must Go On

"Class," said Ms. Hopkins, "I've finished the casting for Washington High's school play."

Dorothy opened a book in front of her face. *If Ms. Hopkins can't see me,* thought Dorothy, *maybe she'll forget about me.*

Dorothy peeked out from behind her book to look at Glenda Poole. *She'll get the leading role*, thought Dorothy. *Even when she's not on stage, she's acting.*

"This year," Ms. Hopkins announced, "the leading role will be played by Dorothy Kipness."

Before Dorothy could stop it, a groan escaped from her lips, "Ohhh, nooo!"

The class laughed, and Dorothy felt her face grow hot and red. Dorothy wanted to say something, but Ms. Hopkins was already reading out the rest of the cast list. "Dennis Morgan will play Fred Johnson. Frank Hogarth will play the policeman. Glenda Poole will play . . ."

As soon as the homeroom bell rang, Dorothy headed straight for Ms. Hopkins. But Glenda got to Dorothy before Dorothy could get to Ms. Hopkins. "Congratulations, Dorothy!" said Glenda. "You'll be great! I just know it!"

Don't give me that, Glenda! thought

Dorothy. *You're so jealous, you can't see straight.* And Dorothy walked right by Glenda without a word.

"What is it, Dorothy?" asked Ms. Hopkins, looking up from her work.

"Well, Ms. Hopkins," stammered Dorothy. "It was nice of you to give me the lead in the play, but I think that Glenda would do a much better job."

"Why, Dorothy!" exclaimed Ms. Hopkins. "What makes you say that?"

"You know how shy I am, Ms. Hopkins. I couldn't possibly learn all those lines, much less get up in front of the whole school and say them! And Glenda is such a natural-born actress."

"I happen to think that you have a lot of acting talent. And besides, you're much more like the heroine, Nelly Peachtree, than Glenda."

"But, Ms. Hopkins!"

"No buts about it, Dorothy," said Ms. Hopkins. "Here's your copy of the script. I'll see you at play practice today after school."

Dorothy took the script and looked at the title, *She Reached the Stars — The Nelly Peachtree Story.*

Ha! thought Dorothy. *By the time I get through with this play, it will be called,* She Fell on her Face — The Dorothy Kipness Story.

The play was about a shy girl who ended up as president of a large oil company. As Dorothy started to read through it, she could see why Ms. Hopkins had cast her as Nelly Peachtree. *She is like me*, thought Dorothy. But that only made her feel more embarrassed.

After school, when Dorothy walked into the auditorium for play practice, the first person she saw was Glenda.

"I'm sorry about this morning, Glenda," said Dorothy. "I was just upset about playing the lead."

"Sure, Dorothy," said Glenda, "I bet."

Dorothy could see that Glenda was really jealous. "No, really, Glenda. I would be much happier if *you* were playing Nelly Peachtree. You know how much I hate to get up in front of people."

"Uh, huh," said Glenda, not believing a word Dorothy said.

"Oh, forget it," said Dorothy, as she realized that there was no use in talking to Glenda.

Ms. Hopkins had everyone sit around a table and read the play aloud. It was a funny play. Nelly Peachtree was one of those people who just seemed to have a lucky star. Time after time, whenever it looked as if Nelly had made a big mistake, it turned out all right. In the play, it was Nelly's shyness that helped her. Everyone else in the oil company would speak too soon. But Nelly, by waiting until last, always came up with the right answer. By the end of the play, Nelly had become president of the world's largest oil company.

The cast members sitting around the table laughed as they read the play. Dorothy felt a little better after the first day of practice. But her good feeling didn't last very long. The next day, the cast had to get up on stage and walk around while they practiced.

Every time Dorothy said a line, Ms. Hopkins would yell from the back of the auditorium, "Louder, Dorothy! I can't hear you!"

Dorothy would try the line again.

Ms. Hopkins would yell from the back of the auditorium, "Louder, Dorothy! I can't hear you."

NELLY. I've finished the job, Mr. Johnson.

"Louder!" Ms. Hopkins would shout.
Dorothy couldn't believe it. She felt
she was shouting. Finally, Dorothy
tried her line one more time.

NELLY. I've finished the job, Mr. Johnson.

"Say it louder!" cried Ms. Hopkins.
Now Dorothy was mad. "I'm saying it
as loud as I possibly can!" she yelled at
the top of her lungs.
The whole room grew quiet. Dorothy
realized that she had just shouted at
Ms. Hopkins.
"Perfect!" laughed Ms. Hopkins.
"*That* I could hear! Now say your lines
that loud."

From that moment on, Dorothy knew what loud meant. She knew how to make herself heard.

For three weeks, they worked on that play. When Dorothy wasn't in school or at play practice, she was learning her lines. But as each day passed and opening night grew closer, Dorothy became more and more nervous.

Finally opening night arrived. Dorothy walked around school in a daze.

All those people will be watching me! she thought. *There's no way I can do it!*

Dorothy got to the auditorium about an hour before the play was supposed to start. She went to the dressing room to put on her make-up.

But while Dorothy was busy with her make-up, Glenda was playing a trick on her. She got one of Dorothy's high-heeled shoes from the costume closet, took a knife, and loosened the heel!

Glenda put the shoe back just before Dorothy came into the room.

"Break a leg!" said Glenda as Dorothy put on her shoes.

Soon the lights in the auditorium went down. The music began to play, and the curtain went up. Dorothy's stomach was doing flip-flops.

The first actor went out on stage and said his lines. Dorothy didn't go on until five minutes into the first act. She listened and waited for her cue.

MR. JOHNSON. If we can't find some unusual person to take over, our company will lose millions of dollars!

MABEL. I know one person who can take over—Nelly Peachtree!

MR. JOHNSON. Well, send her in at once!

MABEL. Nelly! Come here at once!

That was her cue. Dorothy took a deep breath and walked onto the stage. She wobbled as she walked. *Boy!* thought Dorothy to herself. *I must be nervous!*

Dorothy walked over to the actor playing Mr. Johnson and said her first line.

NELLY. Mr. Johnson . . .

Then Dorothy started to walk over to the window, but her feet were still wobbling. Suddenly, in front of all those people, she fell down and landed in one big heap!

The entire auditorium was silent. The other actors were stunned and surprised. Dorothy didn't know what had happened until she looked down at her shoes and saw her broken heel.

That awful Glenda! thought Dorothy. *I'm sure she has something to do with this!*

But Dorothy pulled herself together, got up, and dusted herself off. She looked the actor playing Mr. Johnson right in the eye and said her line.

NELLY. That's right, Mr. Johnson. I may not be able to walk very gracefully, but I'm the unusual person you need to run this company!

Then Dorothy took another step and, on purpose this time, went crashing to the floor.

The audience loved it! They began to laugh and clap. From that moment on, they loved everything that Dorothy said and did. Dorothy felt better and better. She had never had so much fun in

*Dorothy looked the actor playing Mr. Johnson
right in the eye and said her line.*

her entire life. She loved it!

After the play, the audience stood and applauded Dorothy. The next day, everyone was talking about how funny Dorothy had been, especially when she fell down.

And Glenda? Well, she learned her lesson and told Dorothy how she had tried to trick her.

"I'm sorry, Dorothy," said Glenda. "I was jealous, and everybody knows it now."

"That's O.K.," said Dorothy. "If it hadn't been for you, who knows? The play could have been a big flop!"

Glenda looked at Dorothy for a minute, then they both laughed.

"Come on, Dorothy," said Glenda. "Let me buy our shy star a soda."